For friend, writer and polar bear whizz David Bedford,
and Kate, Isobel and Tom - P.L.

For all polar bears and the people who work to protect them - G.H.

First published in Great Britain in 2008
This edition published 2015
Deepdene Lodge, Deepdene Avenue,
Dorking, Surrey, RH5 4AT, UK
www.bonnierpublishing.com

Printed and bound in China

ISBN: 978 1 84812 500 1 (paperback)

1 3 5 7 9 10 8 6 4 2

Best Friends Or Not?

Paeony Lewis · Gaby Hansen

PICCADILLY PRESS · LONDON

Nanook and Suka were best friends.

Splat! Splat! Splat!

They always played snowballs together.

Nanook splashed into the sea.
"Hello seals," he said.

They all swam to the icebergs, where
Suka wouldn't go, and played chase
until it was time for the seals
to have their nap.

Splosh!

Nanook waved goodbye to the sleepy seals. "I'll do some exploring on my own," he said.

Slowly, Nanook crept into the mysterious ice cave that Suka wouldn't explore.

Deep inside, something sparkled. There were hundreds of icicles!

Nanook wished Suka could see them too.

DING DANG DONG!
Nanook played musical icicles.
And soon he wasn't alone.

Two Arctic
fox cubs stopped
and sang to
his twinkling
music before
going on their
way.